WHY THE
SEA IS SALT

WHY PEOPLE COME
IN DIFFERENT COLOURS

ORCHARD BOOKS
96 Leonard Street, London EC2A 4RH
Orchard Books Australia
14 Mars Road, Lane Cove, NSW 2066
ISBN 1 86039 700 X (hardback)
ISBN 1 86039 867 7 (paperback)
First published in Great Britain in 1998
Text © Margaret Mayo 1995
Illustrations © Tony Ross 1998
The rights of Margaret Mayo to be identified as the author
and Tony Ross as the illustrator of this work
have been asserted by them in accordance with
the Copyright, Designs and Patents Act, 1988.
A CIP catalogue record for this book is available
from the British Library.
Printed in Great Britain

WHY THE SEA IS SALT

WHY PEOPLE COME IN DIFFERENT COLOURS

RETOLD BY MARGARET MAYO
ILLUSTRATED BY TONY ROSS

ORCHARD BOOKS

WHY THE
SEA IS SALT

When the world was first made, the
water in the sea was fresh and not the
least bit salty. And it would be like that
today, if King Frodi had not been so
greedy and unkind.

In the long-ago times, Frodi, King of the Northlands owned some magic millstones. They looked the same as other millstones that ground up oats or barley. Just two round, heavy stones. It was said, however, that the stones could grind out whatever the owner wished, if he knew how to make them turn.

Kind Frodi was forever saying, "If only I could turn those millstones, I would grind out so many good things for my people! They would all be happy and peaceful and rich!"

Then one day two tall golden-haired women, dressed in long white flowing robes, came to see King Frodi. They were powerfully built, like giants, and yet they were splendidly beautiful.

"And what can I do for you?" asked the king.

"Nothing!" answered the two women.
"We have come to do something for you!
We know how to make the magic
millstones turn!"

Then the king was a happy man. "Bring the millstones!" he called to his servants. "Set them up here! Quickly!"

"What shall we grind for you?" asked the two women when the millstones were finally brought in. "Think carefully!"

"Grind peace and happiness for my people," cried the king. "And some gold too."

"These are good wishes," said the two women.

They touched the magic millstones. "Grind, grind! Peace and happiness for the people!" they chanted "And gold too! Grind on! Grind on!"

From that moment, there was happiness and peace among all the king's people, throughout the land. But King Frodi didn't know about that, because he didn't move out of the room. He just sat there, watching the grains of bright yellow gold pour out from between the stones and pile up on the floor. He had never seen so much gold in one place before – and he wanted more of it, lots more!

After a while the two women said, "Now it is time for us to rest!"

"No!" cried King Frodi, "Keep grinding! Keep grinding!"

So the two women kept on chanting, and the heap of gold grew bigger.

The king could not keep his eyes off it. "I want enough gold to fill the room," he thought. "No, enough to fill the castle. No, the city. Lots and lots of gold."

But as the two women grew tired, they chanted more slowly, and the gold only trickled out. Then the king was angry.

"Why did you come to the castle if you did not wish to grind for me?" he said. "Grind faster! Faster!"

Then the two women chanted faster, and the grains of bright yellow gold began to pour out again. All day they kept on chanting and grinding, and all day the king watched.

When evening came the two women said, "We are very tired. We must rest for a while."

But the sight of so much gold had changed the king. "You may rest for as long as it takes to say 'King Frodi!'" he said. "Listen: 'King Frodi!' There, you have rested. Now grind away. Faster! Faster!"

"King Frodi is no longer a good man,"
said one of the women. "He is greedy
and unkind."

"He must be destroyed!" said the other.
Then they chanted, "Grind, grind!
Strong, fierce warriors to fight King Frodi.
Grind on! Grind on!"

And warriors, all fully armed, leapt out
from between the millstones. Ten ...
twenty ... thirty of them! They surrounded
the king, and with their sharp swords,
they killed him.

But what then? Here was a band of fierce warriors in a country that had been given peace and happiness.

"We can't stay here!" declared the fiercest of the warriors. "Come! Let's take the women and the magic millstones and sail away to another land. Then we shall have everything we want."

So the warriors took the millstones and the tall golden-haired women. They boarded a ship and ordered the sailors to set sail, and when the sailors saw the warriors's fierce and awful strength, they had to obey.

When the ship was some distance out at sea, the fiercest warrior said to the two women. "Now turn the millstones, and show us what you can do!"

"We are tired," they said. "Let us rest for a while."

"Rest? You shall have no rest! Grind on!" ordered the warrior. "Grind what you like! Salt! Anything! But grind on! Grind on!"

Then the two women touched the millstones. "Grind, grind!" they chanted. "Salt! More salt! Grind on! Grind on!"

And pure white grains of salt poured out from between the stones, until there was a huge pile of salt on the deck.

"That's enough!" cried the fierce warrior. "Quite enough! Stop!"

But the two women only chanted faster and faster, and the salt flowed out over everything and everyone, and the ship began to sink. Even then they went on chanting, faster and faster. "Grind, grind! Salt! More salt! Grind on! Grind on! And never cease from grinding!"

And the weight of the salt was so great that the ship sank below the water and down, right down to the bottom of the sea, taking with it the millstones and everyone on board.

Those magic millstones are still lying there at the bottom of the sea, and they are still grinding. So that is why the sea is salt.

(A Scandinavian story)

WHY PEOPLE COME IN DIFFERENT COLOURS

Have you ever wondered why children come in all sorts of different colours? Well, have you? It's because of something that happened long ago.

In that far-off time, there was no earth and it was always dark. But high above the black night sky, in a place that was full of light, lived Nyame, the Sky God. And inside Nyame there lived some spirit people.

Now Nyame liked making things, and a time came when he decided to make something very special. First he took an enormous basket and filled it with earth and planted it with every kind of wonderful plant. But that was not enough for Nyame. He then made lots of splendid animals and birds and insects, and set them among the plants.

When he had finished, Nyame stood back and admired his earth basket. "That's certainly something special!" he said, "and I know exactly where I'm going to put it!"

He carefully cut a round hole in the sky, and then he made a trap door that fitted the hole. He opened the trap door. He tied a rainbow rope to the basket and lowered it through the hole, down and down, until it reached the place where the earth basket is today.

Light flooded through the hole and lit
up everything down below – and that hole
is the round sun, which still lights up the
earth when Nyame's trap door is open.

Nyame was pleased with his work, and he looked down and admired it some more. But after a while he closed the trap door, and immediately it was black night down on the earth basket. "Oh, my poor animals!" said Nyame. "I had forgotten about them! They will be so frightened in the dark!"

There and then, he cut some extra holes in the sky – and those holes are the moon and stars, which still shine when Nyame's trap door is shut.

Nyame was fond of his earth basket, and he was constantly opening the trap door and looking down. Sometimes one or two of the spirit people who lived inside him would climb up into his mouth, and then they would look down as well.

One day, when Nyame was admiring his earth basket, he noticed a bare patch where nothing was growing. "I must fill that up!" he said.

So he took a small basket, the same size as the empty space, and he filled it with plants. He tied a rainbow rope to the basket, and then began to lower it through the hole in the sky.

Now one of the girl spirits who lived inside Nyame was called Iyaloda. She was lively and interested in just about everything. As soon as she heard that Nyame was lowering a small basket, she said to the boy spirit who was her special friend. "Let's go and have a look!"

"Hmmm ... all right," he said. And, hand in hand, they crept up inside Nyame.

When they came to his mouth, Iyaloda and the boy spirit tiptoed over this tongue, up to this teeth and leant out over his big lips. And the next moment Nyame *sneezed*! and Iyaloda and the boy spirit were whirled out of his mouth, down through the hole and **plump** into the middle of the small basket.

By the time they had got their breath back, the small basket had landed and somehow fitted itself into the empty space in the earth basket.

"That was a bit unexpected," said Iyaloda. "But now we are here let's look around."

The two of them set off, hand in hand.

At first they were quite happy. There were so many wonderful things to see. But it was not long before they began to wonder how they could get back to their home inside Nyame. They thought and thought, but they could not think of a way to reach the trap door up in the sky. And then they felt sad.

When darkness came, and the moon and the stars began to shine, they made a shelter with some branches, curled up close to one another and fell asleep.

As the days went by, Iyaloda and the boy spirit often felt real, deep-down sad. It was lonely living by themselves, far away from Nyame and all their spirit friends. Sometimes the boy spirit would wander off and comfort himself by talking to the wind and the trees, and then dancing a lonesome dance. But when Iyaloda, the girl spirit, felt sad, she sat and thought, and she thought. At last, one

day, she had a really clever thought.

When the boy spirit came back, Iyaloda was excited. She said, all in a rush. "I have had a really clever thought."

"Iyaloda," sighed the boy spirit. "I don't want to hear it. Your clever thoughts always lead to trouble. Remember the last one ...'Let's creep up into Nyame's mouth'. That's how we got sneezed down here!"

"This is a sensible thought," said Iyaloda. "Listen, we could make some little ones. Like us. We could call them children. Then we wouldn't be lonely any more."

"And how could we do that?" asked the boy spirit.

"We could dig out some clay and make little models that looked like us and bake them in a fire. Then we could breathe life into them."

"I suppose," said the boy spirit slowly, "I suppose it wouldn't do any harm to try..."

"Let's start making them now," said Iyaloda.

So they dug out clay and made models of little boy children and little girl children, rather like themselves. Then they built a big pile of wood round the models and set it alight.

But Iyaloda was impatient, and it wasn't long before she said, "They must be ready now. Let's look!" and she covered the fire with big green leaves to dampen it down.

When everything was cool, she took out the clay models. Some were pale white, some were pinkish white and some were creamy white. Each one a little different.

"Oh, they are beautiful!" said Iyaloda.
"Let's make some more!" So the next day
they dug more clay, made more models,
built a fire and set it alight.

"This time," said Iyaloda, "I shall bake them for a good while longer and see what happens."

She waited and she waited, and that was something Iyaloda found hard to do. But at last she decided the models had had a long enough bake, and she covered the fire with leaves.

When everything was cool, she took out the models. This time some were deep black, some were rich dark brown and some were reddish brown. Each one a little different.

"Oh, they are beautiful!" said Iyaloda. "Let's make some more!" So the next day they made more models, and set the fire alight again.

"This time," said Iyaloda, "I won't give them a short bake or a long bake. They shall have an in-between bake!"

She waited, and as soon as she thought the models had been baked for an in-between time, she covered the fire with leaves.

And when she took out these models, some were golden yellow and some were golden brown. Each one a little different.

"Oh, they are beautiful!" said Iyaloda. "Let's make. . ."

"No!" said the boy spirit. "We have enough children already! The time has come to breathe life into them."

Then they knelt down and breathed life into each one in turn, and each little clay model came to life, like children waking from a long sleep. So the boy spirit and Iyaloda, the girl spirit, became the first father and the first mother and, because they had their big family to look after and love, they never again felt lonely.

And, of course, from those first children came all the children of the world, in all their different and beautiful colours.

(A West African story)